AuthorHouse™ UK Ltd.
500 Avebury Boulevard
Central Milton Keynes, MK9 2BE
www.authorhouse.co.uk
Phone: 08001974150

This book is a work of non-fiction. Unless otherwise noted, the
author and the publisher make no explicit guarantees as to the
accuracy of the information contained in this book and in some

©2008 Roy Peters. All rights reserved.

No part of this book may be reproduced, stored in
a retrieval system, or transmitted by any means
without the written permission of the author.

First published by AuthorHouse 8/14/2008

ISBN: 978-1-4343-9044-8 (sc)

Printed in the United States of America
Bloomington, Indiana

This book is printed on acid-free paper.

MICROCOSMIC GIRL AND THE SYMBIOTIC NECKLACE

Roy Peters

authorHOUSE®

CONTENTS

The Glowining Mole Face 1
The Adriod Pricne 21
The Symbotic Chamber 31
The Time Portal Doorway 45
The Interlact Spacecraft 53
The Dwarf Slaves 57
The Friendly Giant 65
Seebrace Mountain 73
The Raven In The Night's Sky 81

01
THE GLOWINING MOLE FACE

There lived a girl who would spend each day looking at mirror crying her eyes out each and every morning due to the spots and light beams coming all round her body while looking at mirror each morning she would burst out into tears and one such morning

Abigail lived with parents who worried a lot about her as spent lots of times just crying so one morning she went to the bathroom.

She gazes at a mirror at wonders to herself 'why why am I so ugly and different from other girls and why cant I be normal like other girls who are my age who are attractive and don't have lights coming around their body' she moans to herself loudly with deep sobs in while she looks at the bathroom mirror.

she takes out a tissue and wipes her tears from her eyes and cheeks as she looks at the mirror at the glow on her face and the large black mole that's on her left cheek that's the size of a fifty pence piece also she the pink acne spots on her face and she looks at the mirror she sobs into a white tissue with tears in her bright blue eyes and tears run down her cheeks as her mother calls her to get ready to go school.

'abbey abbey its time for school or you will be late" says her mother

Abigail flickers her very long blonde fair hair which hides her ears as she looks at her face in the mirror including her bright blue eyes and says to herself 'I can't go to school with a big light glow on my face and body and a big mole and these spots I have on my face and braces on my teeth which are horrid as I wish I was attractive like the models in the fashion magazines that mum buys or as a very beautiful Hollywood actress and what I would do to be attractive like them '.

as what will children at my new school say about me as I am sure they will bully me like they did at primary school as I have lights around my body big ears, a mole and spots on my face and these things in my teeth as well' She sobs and talks to herself very quietly not wanting her mother to hear who over as her mother Pam fryler a short slim fair haired woman knocks on the door of their detached house at 23 Bloomsford road, little Venice London. Who is married to Tim fryler a company managing director of a top international merchant bank her mother Pam works as a department store manageress?

'Abigail can you hear me as I you again speaking to your self as its time for school as its your first day your new school as your father and I have paid lots of money to send you to manourbrock as it's a good all girls school and I spent my time their years ago also my sister Hilary went their to and so did my cousins Stephanie and Joan as the boys in your dads side of the family usually go to Eaton and the girls to gordonstone as boarders in the boarding schools but me you and your dad have thought hard and well over this as we want you as a day pupil at manourbrock is a day school and we could not bear to have you away from us at evenings and weekends due to you needing lots of care due to ontore condition you suffer from'

So Abigail opens the door and her mum looks at the angelic glow on her face, which is a beam of light on her face as well as her body...

Her glowing faces and body which make her almost angelic or fairy type as she omit light beams around her body.

She is the first of her kind a glowing mutant or human sized wingless fairy the scientists and doctors who treat her call ontore or mythical historians call elve as she is first of her kind to be seen on earth for centuries but her parents have brought her to all the specialist medical doctors to find a cure and spent tens of thousands on their daughter to find a cure to stop the glow but they can't for Abigail..

As Abigail is adopted by the frylers as she was left there by a strange woman who turned into a dove when she was a baby.

The school she is going to is an all girls private secondary school her parents pay for.

So her mother looks at the light beam coming from her body which glows even more the minute her mother raises a smile at her and hugs her.

Abigail sheds tears as she fears for her first day at school and being bullied not just for her glow which she can not control over but for the very large mole on her face on her left cheek also pink acne spots on her face as well as the braces she has to wear on her teeth all of which make her look very ugly as she is very plain looking and she is medium built and as she lacks confidence in herself as in well being as suffers a lot from very extremely low self esteem as she hates herself for being very ugly as times she day dreams of being a beautiful princess as she fantasies at times of being very beautiful.

So her mother waits at the door way of the front doom. 'Ok Abigail its time now as I wish I could drop you off but I have to be work today as we have a stock take today in the store and I hoped your dad would drop you off at school but has board meeting today and is tied up in work today and t I m not sure its what you really want as you older enough to travel to school now by yourself without me or your dad dropping you off as you can by yourself take the bus to Swiss cottage by your self as you are eleven years old and growing up very fast and I am proud of you' her mother says.

So she heads past her mother who follows her down to Clifford road were the bus stop is which is in Clifton road were she waits for ten minutes and her mother hands her a five pound note to buy her lunch with and she kisses her on the cheeks as the number forty six bus comes

'Here we are and please be good as we have paid for you to go to manourbrock' her mother says as the number forty six bus comes which is a single Decker bus she shows her Childs travel photocard to the driver of the bus as it has her date of birth on it and when she reaches her eighteenth birthday the expiry date of were she has to pay bus fares as an adult..

She sits at the back weeping to herself she moans to her self and takes out a small mirror from her school handbag and tears roll down her face as she sees her glow come back

'If only I was normal again if only mum and dad would not fuss over me and not treat me like a baby as its not my fault this thing happened and any way I am sick of being told it will be ok as I'm not ok and far from it as I hope I can make some friends as I have never had any friends apart from my pet dove metra who can talk very well and she glows like me as she was affected by the accident as well.

As I keep her in the loft were mum and dad cant get to her and what wail they do to a talking bird which omits light she has been affected by this thing as well and if only she was more human instead of a talking over I would at least have a human friend'

So the bus is empty when she gets on and soon gets full up as its gets to st John 's wood and she sees two girls from the school she is going to with navy blue jumpers on, yellow blouses, navy blue skirts and black tights for school.

Uniform who are fifth year girls from her school and in as the 46 bus moves past St. John's wood into fincley road.

She sees a red haired bushy haired girl who is fat with the same school uniform as her come on board eating a bar of chocolate and bites a bit slow lily like mice into her large bar of chocolate and Abigail looks at her and smiles as the bus approaches Swiss cottage tube station.

The two older girls get off the bus followed by Abigail and the red haired fat girl then asks one of the older girls are heading off to manourbrock as 'are heading to manourbrock school its my first day and I cant remember how to get their as it was more than a year ago since I visited it.

The girls take no notice of the red haired fat girl and one girl a dark haired girl just points and laughs at her 'hey fatso you have to find your own way to school as after all it's a school for the privileged and not for the dumb as do you have problem with remembering things as am sure we will see to it that you don't miss registration but it will cost you a bit to on how to get to school.

As we are none for our enterprises and see you are a customer as I want you to hand over your money fatso'

At that Abigail waits behind the fat girl and loess her temper with the tall dark haired girl 'she won't give you her money as she needs it and any way I am on my way to school as I remember how to get their and I will show you how to get their as I if I remember the bus goes near by'

'Hey mole face freak with the light on your face speak please speak when you are spoken to as I hate being spoken to like that as it will cost you' at that the tall brunette girl shoves Abigail to the fall and she gazes her head on the pavement which is across the road from the Odeon cinema and outside the KFC.

A strange man with pin stepped suite and bowler hat sees whets happening as the two girls jenny maycourt the tall dark haired girl and Vicky banks a blonde haired tall girl who is has short hair compared to jenny pull at pulls her hair

'Hey freak show stop shinning the way you do as we have seen you on TV and don't you look as ugly as no boy will ever love you when you get older.

As you are very ugly and you must repeat after me I'M so ugly boys run a mile thanks to my mole face'

Abigail becomes very afraid and the glow on her pretty face starts to disappear .as if she has no powers at all and bravery of just a minute ago of standing up to the older girl goes out of the window.

As the girl taunts her by calling her shinny mole face girl and Abigail repeats the words that the older dark haired girl tells her to

'I'm so ugly and no boy will ever love me as I am so ugly' the tall girl slaps her across the face but she attempts to make her repeat the words over and over again the strange man who has green skin.

Who resembles a frog as he is a frogman mutant yells at the two girls leave her alone before I tell your head teacher and authorities of your evil guise' princess munryeits' 'ok frogman I will stop for now as for you mole face your dead as when we get to school at break time we will make you crawl like a baby as its what we do to freaks like you who don't fit in and are far to dud to go school as for you fatso we are putting you on a diet as I am sure the school nurses will have her work cut out and as for you frogman no one on earth calls me by that name as my name is jenny'

'Isn't you a bit to old for school for a eternal youth girl '

'its none of your business frogman unless you want to fight here on earth to death with my knife as I am not afraid to use it on earth as I am sure freak the humans will want to no who comes they have freaks like frogmen walking about them and killed in cold blood'

At once jenny takes out a blue dagger from her schoolbag and he takes out his until he decided to take out his golden hand laser gun as he forgets his supposed to be on earth on a top secret mission so he points his gun at her and she puts away her knife and he puts his gun back into his jacket 'I will escort you to school as she the princess munryeits cant hurt you while I am round as my name is solrac I am general of earth defence affairs of the united inter cosmic council of federal worlds' so the two bulling girls cross the busy finclely road traffic light crossing.

The strange frogman who shape shifts into human form hands her his business card with three set of phone numbers including a mobile number plus an email address. So the card has a logo of a planet with rings like Saturn with seven stars round it and two

White dove birds side by side on the left and right as the logo appears at the top of the card.

'I am here to protect you from harm and if you ever get into bother with your powers don't hesitate to call me or email me' as he walks away Abigail and the fat red haired girl bushy haired girl walk into fitzjhons avenue were the school is based and he presses a button on his strange blue glowing mobile phone and disappears into thin air..

◆

So the two girls wonder were has disappeared to so then after realising he has gone

Abigail introduces her self to the fat red haired girl and they giggle at the strange man 'my names Abigail fryler and I have not got your name as these girls were cruel calling you fat'

'My friends in my old school call me gorge but my name is Georgina and would you like to be called abbey as after all it is short for Abigail if you don't mind you calling abbey.

So as they enter the school gate they see a thin short girl with dark hair who is sixth former wearing jeans and a white blouse pointing to the direction of were to get to the school assembly hall as they ask her for directions.

So she shows both Abigail and Georgina to the school assembly hall As its were the registration is taking place the school building a an old grey bricked old fashioned Victorian building with a newly modem parts including swimming pool and gym the short girl with red hair shows the two first year girls to were the registration is taking place in the school dinning room on the first floor.

So they go though two set of blue doors and turn left and sees the flight do steps leading to the assembly hall and they see lots of girls sitting down in rows of chairs.

The head teacher miss brigs stands up on the stage with a microphone on the podium and starts her greetings just in time as Abigail and Georgina arrive and four other first years arrive just in time for the start of the school registration to decide which school houses the girls would go in to.

The tall thin Gary haired thin elderly lady takes a look at Abigail and smiles as she recognises her from the media she then speaks with a creaky but soft and loud voice.

'Welcome first years to manourbrock private school for girls and today before we start I want to tell you are few ground rules no one must leave the school gates during break time and also that I like all to be punctual and hand in all home work on time and you must wear school uniform when at school and on school trips during school hours and I do not tolerate those who are absent or late for class or make up excuses like being sick to get a day off school.

Anyway I will read out what form and class and house you will be in as the four houses are named after four famous women of history and they are s charlotte Brunette house. Jane Austin house Emily Pankhurst house and Florence nightingale house and. you will go in to and soon as vie finessed you flow one of the teachers to your class and house you will be in your time at manourbrock'

So the head teacher Starts with class 1b In the charlotte Bronte house and she reads out a list of girls twelve girls in 1a then Abigail name comes out in 1b so those of Georgina Hayes and when she finishes reading out the registration for Abigail's class Mrs Briggs tells the girls in 1b 'please follow miss woods for your first lesson and wait for her while she will hand you all a timetable for this term'

So the twelve girl's inning Abigail and Georgina follow the tall blonde haired woman to the firth floor.

In class Abigail sits next to Georgina Hayes and another girl a black girl called Yvonne Mitchell who looks at the mole on Abigail's face as Miss Wood writes on the white board her name.

'Does it your mole hurt as I have a scare on my left arm caused by a dog that bit me a few days ago' says Yvonne the thin black girl who has long hair that's tied back.

So Abigail responds with smile on her face and then her skin starts to glow as she gets a bit upset and has tears roll down her yes 'no the mole does not hurt but I hate the light coming from my face'

'Wow you the girl in the news the girl with the glow and the mole and anyway my name is Yvonne and my dad wanted me to come here because my older sister carol is in the forth year' says Yvonne.

'Um lets start with the introduction by introducing ourselves as well as the books we like to read and study as in my class every enjoys it and I'm your house master, head of English literature studies. So before we began I go around the classroom as you introduce yourselves.

After I will hand you a copy each of Charles dickens Oliver twist

But for this next six weeks we will be considering this term an essay one with living in Charles dickens Victorian world.

This book is part of your profile on literature essays you will do as part of your overall school marks in this subject we will be also considering the rest of the school year the works of also j.r.r. Tolken and the plays of Oscar Wilde and Shakespeare in this class and before we start can we just introduce your selves while I put a name to a face'

So Miss Wood's points at Abigail 'you start by introducing your self in the middle row and what you like reading or what you want to read as part of your studies'

Woods the youngish teacher whom in her late twenties.

'My name is Abigail fryler and I would like to read Romeo and Juliet as I have herd it's a tragic love story a play by William Shakespeare'

'Thank you Abigail well be doing lots Shakespeare plays and at the start of your third year at this school we do performing arts and we get to do a play or musical as we team with boys school Quentin vale and last year Romeo and Juliet was preformed with the boys school and this year we are doing another school play its midsummer's nights dream which is a Shakespeare play..

Just to mention at the end of each school year there is a school play.

ok I will go around the class to each one of you as you tell me your name and what you have read or would like to read'

So the girls in the class all introduce themselves until Miss Woods hands them a copy of Charles dickens Oliver twist.

So the bell rings for the next lesson which is chemistry and Abigail while walking down the stairs bumps into jenny maycourt as she looks into her mirror.

'Cant you watch were you are going spot face as wait till break time as you will be dead and stop looking at that mirror in your hand as it may crack' as she moves on jenny shoves Abigail to the side of the sitar case.

So Abigail walks to the third floor were the science lab classroom is she sees a spectacled brown hair woman called Miss Ripley near the black board.

Abigail looks forward to that class but the teacher makes the lesson very boring by having them copy from the black board of what happens when chemicals are mixed together like house hold cleaning products bleach and a cleaning product.

They don't get to experiments with chemicals in this lesson but Miss Ripley gives them homework to do write an essay on how safe-cleaning products can become dangerous if mixed with other household cleaning products.

So at break time Abigail and Georgina head outside and see jenny maycourt and her friends Vicky

Taylor with another girl curly haired fair girl none as Sandra banks.

The three girls giggle and point at Abigail and jenny takes out a cigarette from a packet from her school bag and calls Abigail over 'hey mole face come try one of these if you don't to want to hurt as lets see if the smoke comes out of your mole'

Abigail being very terrified of jenny and the two girls starts to cry and they and then jenny lights up the cigarette while a short brown haired school teacher who is on break duty is not looking in the playground which is full of girls and some playing netball and hanging about in the playground.

'Watch this girls as lets watch this freak have smoke come from her mole as hold it then mole face and just puff into it as its nice for you'

At that Abigail drops the cigarette as she refuses to smoke it but then jenny slaps her across the face and pulls at her long blonde hair which is tied in a brace like a ponytail and tells her to lick her shoes and pick up the cigarette and smoke it.

Georgina looks on with fear on her face as jenny puts the cigarette in Abigail's mouth and then Abigail coughs out and spits out the cigarette

'Well it shows you mole face that we girls are clever. to be clever you need to liven up a bit as you are a walking freak show and I want you to crawl on the floor as if you don't I will rip the hair of your head and repeat after me.

I am an ugly mole face and I am so stupid that I will lick the shoes of every girl in the playground, as I want you must repeat what I said and lick my shoes with your tong as now I will take you to the girl's toilet.

For our welcome to manourbrock initiation ceremony as you still must repeat what I have to say I am a ugly mole face girl who is so stupid that I need extra classes to learn'

So Abigail repeats the words 'I am a ugly mole face who is stupid that I need extra classes 'at that jenny gives her a shove to the floor and holds her head and makes her lick the her shoes and shoes Vicky's and Sandra 's with her tong and Abigail does what jenny tells her as she is very terrified of her..

'very good lick up my shoes as whets you are good at freak as make my shoes shine right now with the light on your face or I will take you to the girls toilet'

So jenny, Vicky and Sandra hold on to Abigail who is sobbing her eyes out and they take her to the girls toilet on the ground floor into a toilet cubicle and jenny gets Abigail's hair and shoves down the toilet bowl and flushes the toilet and water goes all over her very beautiful long blonde fair hair of which jenny unties..

As Abigail bursts into tears a teacher passing by as in Miss Woods gets to hear what is happening as Abigail screams with tears on her eyes.

At that Miss Woods enters the toilets and sees the three bullies holding the first year girl down the toilet bowl.

'Jenny what have I told you about bulling and Mrs Briggs wont be palisades with you as you her ace student who should not be bulling as you have be warned time and again'

'But miss she is felling very sick and we had to help her as its first day nerves as I remember my first day here '

The girls move away as Abigail sobs to her self and vomits as the fear of being bullies makes her sick.

" Are you ok Abigail as you look under the weather and you will tell me if you have been bullied by theses fifth years as what was they doing to you as your hair is wet and anyway I will get a dry owl for you from the staff room from my bag'

'Its fine I will be ok' says Abigail but miss woods insists on the owl and Abigail flours her to the staff room and she tells Abigail to wait outside while she hands a large white owl to dry her hair with.

The staff room is on the ground floor next to the new part of the building is the swimming pool and gym is and indoor netball court is.

So Abigail Dries her hair with the towel and Miss Woods takes Abigail to the school nurse, which is a room on the fourth floor, was sick bay is.

So miss woods expanse to the school nurse miss vaquero that she had been sick in the toilet and she will need to rest a bit before they contact her parents to take her home.

So miss woods leaves laves her in the medical room with the school nurse who puts thermometer under her throat to cheek her temperature 'ok I cant give you any thing In case you are allergic to it. But your temperature is ok and as for your mole I subject you get your parents to see your GP about some kind of cream.

As for the light on your face well it's a rarity and I have seen on TV and I am sure they will be a cure but I am not sending you home for the day I am writing to your GP. So please hand this note to the headmistress as I'm sure its nothing but a stomach bug'

Abigail then burst into tears as she fears she may be bullied again as she hears jenny coming to the medical room complaining of a headache but it's a lie as she wants to cheek weather Abigail has told on her for making lick shoes.

So jenny knocks on the door and the school nurse says wait a minute while I deal with some one.

So the nurse to either wait gives Abigail the choice for her parents to take her home or stay at school for the day, as after all it was Abigail's first day at her new school.

So she comes out of the medical room and sees jenny who gives her a evil sitar and points at the mole on her face and whispers to Abigail

'I told you the nurse would have her work cut out mole face as I will see you later at lunch time and don't forget if you tell me on me I will cut your hair off and make you beg for mercy.

So Abigail heads to the ground floor were the head teachers room is and hands a note paper while knocking the door to the headers Mrs Briggs who is reading the times newspaper and Abigail knocks the door and the headmistress lets her in.

'So Abigail fryler you are feeling ill and it's only your first day well what is relay bothering you as you will tell me if its problems at home or with our style of teaching or is the fact that you are tied of fame.

As I cant have out of school not when the nurses put down to first day nerves. As this is a school of excellence and what would your parents think if I were to send you home or call them on your first day as I want you to remain at school the reminder of the day

. As in this school we don't do sick as parents like yours pay a lot of money and if you think you rather be in a state school then take out with them no lets look at your timetable to see were you are supposed to be.

So she takes out her timetable out of her school handbag and hands it to Mrs Briggs who looks at it.

'I see before lunch you have geography with Mrs curshshaw and you better be their as you are late and if you feel any worse please see your house master who must authorise this before I can give the go ahead for you to go home you being out of class to see me and to go home ill as it's the rules here as do I make myself clear to you as you are to in future are to in form your house master before I can let you go home'

'I understand Mrs Briggs and I am sorry 'so Mrs Briggs picks up her times newspaper and looks in the dark blue yes of Abigail fryler who is upset but holding back tears as the headmistress refuses to send her home as well as call her parents she is ill.

'You are bright girl miss fryler and I hate to have see you in my office for sickness as in this school we don't get sick we strive for experience as your mother and aunt who I taught was exhalant students and I hope you can achieve what your mother and aunt did when here so you better head off to class as you have misses more than half of your geography lesson'

At that Abigail slams the door with anger not as if she hated school but it was the bullying she hated and by also a head teacher who did not like her and had her one she liked as jenny was one of her favourites.

So the day goes by with out any incident as she spent her time crying and hiding in the girls toilets eating a cheese sandwich for lunch she brought in the school canteen her friend Georgina was busy chatting to other girls and ignored again as many girls choose to ignore Abigail or either make snide remarks about her face.

She after school she takes the bus home and when she arrives she see `s a weird looking boy outside her flat holding a clipboard.

02
THE ADRIOD PRICNE

So Abigail wonders why the boy a black boy looks so weird looking and is smiling at her and speaking into a Dictaphone.

He approaches her as she try to enter her door the boy a half android with metal arms looks wearing very weird brown robes stands next to her 'I am sorry to disturb you but I have come from the future and come Abigail to prepare for your task ahead as I have been noticed today the incident with a very evil dark princess who has disguised herself while on earth to primly mount a invasion baked by her father the emperor zarn'

Abigail opens the door with her keys and looks at the weird dressed black boy in brown robes, which are slaves, and he has metal arm and Afro hair.

'I don't know what you are on about as I will phone the police unless you leave and any way I have had a rotten day and don't need a strange looking boy picking on me'

He then speaks into the Dictaphone as she slams the door on his face 'this superhero is showing signs of fear and she has yet come to realise that she has powers able to defeat the emperor who has Nan powers and is one many hope to end this cosmic war as she has proven in my time line that she can defeat many enemies and how can I convince her that she is to be a superhero the living and legendary microcosmic girl as at this time I will attempt to ring her bell before her parents come home as I will have no other option but to teleprompt later on if all fails with her as how can I convince her that she is special and we in decorian galaxy need her' so the boy puts away his Dictaphone and rings the bell of the big dark blue door which has number 23 on it.

So she answers the door and boy smiles at her and takes from his robes a electronic tape messier machine 'let me measure you so I can have a costume made for you for disguise as the general wants me to measure you and please Abigail let me at least come in as I can understand your first day as when I was at school I use to bullied for being a half android and you told me in the future of how jenny maycourt use to bully you until she found out you was microcosmic girl her deadly foe and you was great in the duel quest contest before the emperors daughter will to take something from you must wear this necklace for your own protection and it will stop the glow.

as In the emperor zarn ruler of anzore empire of worlds and his daughter make you lose you powers and it why am here to here to give you this necklace as it will stop you from dying and you must wear until you older enough to heal the radiation as the necklace is a symbiotic necklace which can heal the radiation poisoning and make live an eternity as once you go into the body merging chamber you will be one with symbiotic necklace and it will be part of you but if you remove you will die within days of removing it as it can stop you from dying and also give you the power to heal others.

but sadly the emperor daughter princess munryeits is back again after you first defeated her once in battle and it why I am to make sure you defeat her once and for all time and stop this cosmic war between the cosmic council of allied worlds and the empire of anzore as in the future the emperor drains all your cosmic powers in the dual quest contest and its why I am here to prepare you for the battles ahead'

At that she slams the door on his face then stands behind the door with tears on her eyes and then changes her mind and opens the door to the boy who smiles at her and hands her a tissue and her gives the necklace which looks unlike anything seen on earth as it comes from the future made by androids..

'You told you get picked on because of your weirdness any way can you stop me from being picked on as I am sure you can as the this strange man who look like a frog earlier on told me to ring him if I had any trouble with jenny and he mentioned something about her being in disguise '

So the boy hands a glowing blue disc which like a dad or CD disc but this disc shines a lot and she looks it and decided to let him in to the living room.

'it must be general solrac a friend of mine as lives in rents house in the sty johns wood location of London anyway According to my data you must Abigail fryler as I have travelled a very long way and from the future to prepare you for the duel with the dark princess munryeits she is very good with a deadly new weapon called a ortlare stick its shaped like a wand but does more evil than witches wand as it make person grow old and die and can only be reversed by placing a persons remains in a resurrection chamber and she is a very dangerous assassin its why I have come from the future

To prepare you for the battle ahead as I am from the fayemoorac in the primus galaxy of the central universe's which ortbeings being call ort alpha one of many universes.'

So Abigail takes a deep look at weird boy whom big Afro hair pointed ears, as he is an android elve and metal arms in a sleeveless robe with a plastic face with blue glowing eyes.

'So you have come to pick on me with your tales of some battle and I have had a very rotten day today as I have picked on by some girls and any way please tell what you want before my parents come home as you look very weird as are you a robot of some kind as I have never seen any one like you before'

'If you mean the hair I mean to cut it but I like it big' says Abigail who can't take her eyes of his metal robotic arms and which are made of steal.

'I mean your arms and the clothing you are wearing as you can't be from around her as you told me are from the future'

'IM a half android as giants and a ape race none Mekong me ripped to pieces and left me for dead as almost my body is android including my brain as the human side of me is no all gone and I cant grow old into adulthood as I have been like this for over three hundred years now and I am use to it now' so he shows his metal legs and metal chest which are robotic as well.

'Do you get picked at school because you are a android as I have a mole on my face, big ears with glasses on and a skin glows so much that at times I have no control over it'

So the boy sits down next to the TV on a red sofa chair and looks at her and smiles and gets off the sofa in the living room which has two doors one to the corridor and one glass door that leads to the patio garden and he looks at glass door and then speaks into his Dictaphone 'the humans have provided a home for our superhero and she is very never and does not yet no of her destiny'

He then puts the Dictaphone away as she approaches him and wonders to herself why he is calling her a superhero.

'Well Abigail as a warrior prince one is used to having enemies and being picked on as you tell in the future about you being bullied by jenny maycourt a vile girl who is no angel but a vile girl who makes your life a misery and its why I am here to prepare you for your destiny as you are living legend in the future as well as the past in many worlds across the universes and I remember the day you came to my world when I was eight years old a mere boy who was not a twelve year old eternal youth android'

So the boys face goes all blank as he dreams about the past the day a costumed Abigail dressed in a green superhero's costume with a helmet visits his world bringing with her the last unicorn none alive anywhere in the universes.

He has smiles on his face as he was in the woods hunting dear for food with his late father king aloft when she approaches them and gives the boy a gift he never forgets as she beings him in Forrest a white golden unicorn the last horse of its type.

He remembers very vividly her outfit which was green tights made of a alien type rubbery type of leather that's silky   with black underwear including bra that's made of rubbery plastic type of metal made from tuncin spiders webs and she on her head wears a metal visor helmet and she he remembers her taking it off to introduce herself as microcosmic girl.

His father induces himself as king alfont and him as Prince Freddie. It was in those days when the land of mernac was kingdom of flairegore before the whole the planet became a principality ruled by a crown prince as part of the inter cosmic federal council of allied worlds.

As his father king alfont is long since passes away so his mother the queen Candice due to the inter galactic as Freddie remembers her dinning with his father the king the day Boer his planet is invaded by a

He sees his father killed in battle while on horse back with sword as a young girl on winged horseback who is an evil immortal princes none kills him in a sword fight.

When he goes back to the town were he lived he sees almost kill all the people dead killed by this dark princess with long dark hair and red skin with scales with fiery red eyes as evil mutant beings from the world of anzore.

His brain shuts down and falls on the floor as his android power fade for a few minutes as he remembers the deep loss he suffered long before he was made warrior crown prince of the planet fayemoorac.

She see him fall to the floor and wakes him up 'are you ok as by the way you seemed ok just now as is it normal for a boy like to faint in front of a girl'

'Well it happened when I think of the past a lot anyway I better introduce myself as my name is Freddie Dothan I'm the exiled crown prince of fayemoorac the last in my families dynasty of nobles Abigail microcosmic girl and have run away to live in ortcosmic city it their we meet up with general solrac and claytor who is a dwarf

boy ' so he smiles at her and she starts to blush and glow like a light bulb with embarrassment and wonders to herself how comes he knows her name and she touches his metal hands and he holds her hands very gently as she chats with him.

'How comes you now my name and why do you call me by that as it's what the newspapers sometimes call me if not the girl with the glow'

He holds her very softly and she feels the warmth of his hands and he keeps quite and his memory goes back a few years into the future when saves his life from princesses munryeits who defeats him in lazier sword duel and she stands in her way and knocks the sword of dark princesses hands with her lazier coming from her hands as princess munryeits rides on a white flying horse on a hill top with Freddie on Gary flying horse.

Freddie remembers that day very well she first defeated the dark elves princess in combat and on another occasion rescues him from drowning abroad a ship sunk by me core's who are the ape people from the earth like planet none as mecore.

He has found memories of the furtive and of the past when he rescues he from being lazier whipped to death by fair haired boy prince none as eubie in the new Rome gladiatorial arena were also giant creatures are let lose on him and he rescues him yet again.

So the prince mind go back to the future the day help free the dwarves from giants who made slaves and helped save a good giant and few friends of their a pack of wolves

So Freebie's mind switch to the present of how he can get her to the future which is doomed as earth is at war with Anzore Empire and the united cosmic federal council of

Allied worlds are close to surrender in the year 100, 045 in far of future.

So Abigail has no idea the reason he has come from the future to see and when he takes out his CD like commuter she finds herself mysteriously in the future of the one hundredth thousand and forty fifth centaury ad.

She finds herself aboard a gigantic space station in a hospital wing on a bed with a cat like looking woman dressed in nurses out fit seeing to her.

03
THE SYMBOTIC CHAMBER

The cat likes woman who is a humanoid cat woman who has ginger whiskers and fur and orange eyes. So the nurse goes into the dressing table in the hospital wing of ortcosmic city which is a gigantic space station in the layntor solar system in the ort mort galaxy in orbit above the planet lyntor the space station is the size of our moon which is the headquarters of the inter cosmic federal council of worlds.

The space stain is round like a moon like planet with lots of towers on it and it glows white in the darkness of space like a rood hedgehog due to the towers it has on it.

For transpiration it has a monorail network and flying cars in it in the glass dome structure that's been built on a moon that's the size of earth.

So Abigail puts on her glasses and gets of the bed and sees the sting cat humanoid woman taking from her draw her school uniform and her handbag.

'We are discharging you now as you have been here for a week in a coma brought

Here by crown prince Freddie who will be waiting for you in fayemoorac as we have ships on trade heading that way and its two day ride way by interstellar standards instead of months and years under the old technology or unless you want to wait in the presidential hotel suite were I is sure presidential councillor Rushmore

will be their to greet you and look after you as the procaine has told me a lot about you and IM one his most trusted aides a private nurse to him and to you as my name Nina paws but some call me just paws as I will show to the Mona rail that heads to the presidential wing.'

Abigail looks all a round her and outside the window were she sees the lots of flying cars in the ceiling sky line of the city dome and she burst into tears.

'Were am I were am I how did I get here and were is again as I want to go home and feed by pet dove metre who can talk like you cat'

So the nurse comforts her and gives her a golden necklace with a round small disc on it with the words transmutation it has a button on it and it's a symbiant electronic being.

'The prince told me to tell you are to press this button when in private and it only works on you as me and only a mere handful no of your identity don't worry I will shut the curtains while you activate the button on the disc that's on the necklace'

So she leaves the private hospital bedroom and then Abigail wonders to herself if this button can cure her mole and stop the glow and to her surprise her body starts to change and she grows a foot taller and sudsy her mole on her face disappears but her glow does not and then suddenly a flash of lighting happens as the computer on the disc tells her Abigail fryler of earth are ready to transmute into microcosmic girl yes or no.

At that Abigail screams and says yes with tears on her eyes and when she does she is transformed in to a superhero with costume on a green silky leather cat suit with helmet and visor.

On her head is helmet and visor is also coloured green and she loses all memory of being Abigail fryler as she is transformed in the first time in her life as microcosmic girl and when she is transformed into her sight improves and she has no need for glasses and the mole on her face disappear as well as the acne spots and braces on her teeth so when she is transformed she becomes almost elve like.

So the nurse responds as she sees her in her new costume 'I will make you into a teleporter of time and space as you will become a elve cosmic warrior of time and space head to the time teleport chamber as its their your body will merge with me and become one person as long as you wear me and you must give this necklace to a new host once you have reached your adulthood as after time you will drink of the

entrap spring waters of tonaz which will make young forever
' says the computerised voice of the symbiotic necklace

So the nurse takes her out to the busy corridor in the hospital then walks her

Of the hospital which is built like a glass crystal skyscraper tower with over fifty driftnet floors. Paws the nurse follows to the symbiotic chamber which can make her in to a shape shifter and make her change into microcosmic girl without having to use her hand to dries

'I am flowing you to the past and anyway the cosmic council military are the ones who mostly have access to the symbiotic chambers which will turn you into time teleporting mutant crime fighting heroine as you must remember you have been chosen to wear the first civilian to wear won in the cosmic council of worlds which earth is an affiliated member not due to become a full member for until 2110 and via time machines and symbiotic chambers that merges your body with it.

So think of earth back then and of the pollution on earth and power drain on your power and its why I am following you to earth to 2007 as I can treat you should you get hurt as many humans back did not take to you back then anyway wont it be safer is you transmute back to her.

'The prince taxed me last night told to take of my necklace as an evil princess wants I have to make her immortal forever'

So they teleport and microcosmic girl presses the button from the year 100,000,201 to the year 2006 London little Venice.

'Take me to September 1 4 the London little Venice please'

The computer on the necklace the lift responds by saying 'afrermetive microcosmic girl we have arched the destination of London little Venice' so the black glass lift takes them on the pathway of the canal of little Venice were the narrow boats are and a café is.

So microcosmic girl comes out and followed by Nina paws who are still dressed in nurse's outfits as they step out the lift distress into thin air as microcosmic girl activates the cloaking device which them invisible to the past Abigail who is looking.

'That's me and I am crying'

'you can not allow your self to be see your self or you will be lost in a time vortex which can affect the balance of the universe your self as it took once four years to come out of the vortex and I still at time see myself from the future leaving ortcosmic city due the city being captured by the anzore empire as ortcosmic city is capital city of the united federal cosmic council of allied worlds or cosmic council for short anyway activate your sibilant necklace to take you to take you back to a safe time in the future were you came from and you will find your self back in the symbiotic chamber '

'Legend says no one knew back who was microcosmic girl who rarely was human or an ortbeings from space' the paws the cat human woman says to microcosmic girl.

"What an ortbeings "says microcosmic girl
'it another means non earthly mutant being"
'I better take you back to the one hundredth thousand centaury were came from and I show you to the council presidents office as he wants to meet you before head off home back to the year 2007'

So Abigail wonders to herself who she can stop the symbiotic necklace from being stolen as it can make her only her into her as into a another being not just any being but a superhero none as microcosmic girl so she is brought back to the year 2007 in September a few minutes after she was transported to the future by prince Freddie so she is back at her at home at number 23 Bloomsbury road feeling very sad due to being bullied on that day and for being chosen to wear the symbiotic necklace.

So in her bedroom and memories of the far off future and of ortcosmic city and off the legendary tales of her fighting villains in many worlds across time.

This thought entering her mind worries her and she remembers the day Freddie Measured up for a costume and it looked like the one the girl was wearing who is her when she changes into microcosmic girl via shape shifting without using her hands

So she rings up general solar on her mobile when she arrives in her bedroom after walking up the stairs as she remembers what he said to her the previous day about ringing him up should she encounter danger from jenny maycourt who is dark princess munryeits and has taken the guise of a earthly human school girl.

So he answers the mobile phone and gets a bit angry at a croaking frog like voice, as he is aboard his space ship the nemesis a long cigar shaped vessels that's cloaked at the other side of the world in Australia.

'Who is this at this time of the night as cant you see I need my sleep anyway who is this'

At that Abigail then sobs to him and tells him what had happened and whom he had left a business card with his number on it.

'I woke up in hospital then you took home with Freddie and today this girl gave me a nucleus with small CD disc on it that has a button and all I remember is that girl who looks like jenny pulling the necklace chain of my neck and I woke up in hospital with you their and you told me to ring you should I get the necklace back and I have but I it seems like one dream as I feel somehow different some how'

So the frogman croaks and then softens his voice to her as he finds out she is upset 'what ever you do not press the button as you will lose all memory of your actions as this device has not been perfected yet and only works with you as you have nano radiation in your blood stream and what vet you do please sit tight while I find out what munryeits wants with the necklace as I can not protract you from yourself as when I have transmutetated I lose all memory of whom I am at times.

 but recently with memory enhance probe I have been able to shape shift without losing my memory or suffering short memory lose as I have seen in you action a few times as microcosmic girl and you make me proud and your parents as you have so far stopped the invasion and anyway abbey stay firm and calm and in sure it will all make sense to you once I get permission from the grand councillor to put a mind probe in your brain anyway it wont hurt but tick as make it 2200 hours tomorrow evening at Hyde park as its were I will meet you to discus our next strategy as I now you better as microcosmic girl and you are more confident as her '

So she is about to speak by saying 'but who is this microcosmic girl' her credits on her phone run out.

The following day she heads to school the normal way taking the number 46 bus to school and when she arrives at school and sees jenny with her two friends Sandra and Vicky and they some how this time ignore as they wait outside the school gates and Abigail sees a rolls Royce car pull over next to the school gates and sees a tall bearded man come out who has bald head who is her father sir Douglas maycourt.

He wears a black suite and dark glasses and Abigail sees the man yelling at her about whom she let that microcosmic girl get away with the neck lass.

Abigail wonders if it's her neck class that he is on about and does her best to hide the neck class under her school uniform under her yellow blouse she wears that day as the day is a warm September day and she does not wear her navy blue school uniform jumper.

She sees Georgina in the playground chatting Yvonne Mitchell and Abigail walks towards them and Yvonne leaves them to chat to another girl.

Georgina hugs Abigail as she sees her and hands her a lollipop in a wrapper as she is sucking one lollypop a green lemon tasting one.

As Georgina gives Abigail a lollypop Abigail responds to her by saying 'no thanks' at that jenny maycourt and her two friends Sandra banks and Vicki Taylor walks in and at once jenny rushed up towards Abigail and within minuets a stage man papers out of nowhere with a note to give a tall Ube skinned man he gives a note to jenny who reads it to herself.

Then the man disappears into thin teleprompting back to a space ship and she touts at him and looks at Abigail and gorging and points to the school gates 'I knees to cheek you too for something as its something I want'

As soon as jenny is about is drag Abigail outside of the school gates the school bell rings for the start of the first lesson.

The lesson is tank by miss swift who tells the class that they should all now their times table by now and in this lesson they will be studying algebra and long diversion and will have home work to do.

So the lesson ends and jenny waits outside the class room for Abigail as she skips her class as she has copy of the first years time table and a tall blue man flowers her about and is dressed in a black suite and wares dark glasses.

The man says to jenny 'we need to start with this class as your father is sure that the girl with the glow and the mole is microcosmic girl the one the Ontore foretell as the conquer of our people as you now what failure means to your father as we must execute her at once if she is found to have the necklace'

So Abigail comes out of the class room with Georgina and as soon as she comes out of class the man puts a bag of her head and lifts her up and then takes her aboard her his space ship followed by jenny who then shape shits into her natural self as princess munryeits.

As soon as she arrives on the dark pyramid shaped spacecraft which is cloaked in orbit kidnapped by the two of them Abigail makes tries to make a run for it.

While in school gorgerin tells the Miss Swift what happens by seeing being bundled into a sack and then despairing into thin air?

When the next lesson happens and the rest of the day happens the police are notified who then contact the inter cosmic council of worlds military police force.

The school is shut down for two days as the cosmic military police look for clues of a teleportation radiation residue.

So on the pyramid space craft Abigail is tied to bed and as jenny attempts to take the necklace from her blouse a strange thing happens as Abigail suddenly finds her self in a strange world with golden brownish tall like trees in the middle of a Forrest with lots of unicorns and she sees a centaur who gets angry at her for appearing out of nowhere.

The centaur is a fair skinned man and he gallops towards her and snaps at her 'I am sedrac the royal keeper of the scared unicorns and what beings you stranger as I have permission by king ramjax to kill any one who mere touches this herd as theses are the last left any were in the universe as the dark princess and her father emperor earn have all but hunted them down to extinction and why are you here stranger'

As she speaks to her face starts to glow and he then stops being aggressive towards her 'you are a Ontore girl a earthling one and what bring you to flairegore'

The censure looks at three girls and raises a smile as he feeds the unicorns with hay.

'I was taken by her from school and I find myself here"

So the contour touches the mole on her face and looks at it with amazement

As he has never seen such a large mole like that before.

'so you say were brought some how by the dark princesses as she is very devious in her grasp for power and I would not put any thing past her to bring you here and its why as a earthling Ontore you must be careful as these are dangerous times we live in young maiden and you must be were it is safe with your peoples as these woods are not safe for mere mortal girl like yourself as you as you are mortal I suppose by the spots on your face and the mole'

So sera points at the mole on her face and she gets very upset and as she starts

to think of jenny maycourt bulling her by calling her spot face as she hated the mole on her face and he comforts her by calling over a unicorn and she stops crying when she starts to stroke the unicorn.

As soon as she touches it the unicorn starts to glow like her skin and she then asks sera if she can ride on it as her parents have taken her horse riding in the past.

Sedrac then looks at her with more amazement as some how her disc on her declass she wears under her uniform has been accelerated.

She starts to grow taller her mole dissipaters and suddenly the computer on the computerised disc declass activates by saying 'transmute nation process in progression to subunit being microcosmic girl'

So within minutes she is transformed into microcosmic girl with full constitute on including helmet.

Sedrac strands aback as she see lots of lightning rays hitting her body and then looks at the superhero girl 'you are the processed one the one foretold long ago and please let me hold the hand of the one they call microcosmic girl'

Microcosm girl then looks at Sedrac and points to the sky 'you must be the keeper of the unicorns as my host is very tied I must take go home before my mortal body gets killed is killed as if she I am killed as mortal I will no longer exist as a immortal warrior'

Within minutes of her speaking microcosmic girl collapses on the floor and changes back into Abigail.

Sedrac picks her up and decides to leave unicorns as he takes the sleepy Abigail on his back and she wakes up all confused.

'what happened just now as a herd a voice in my head saying transmute and now I am back here with you Sedrac'

'I must take you to the king for your safety as you must return home before the dark princess gets to find about your whereabouts and you must head back to earth to your home as it s what you want as microcosmic girl'

So Abigail sitting on the contours back chats to him about what she likes about school apart from the bulling and within minutes a loud ringing sound is herd in the field like a phone ringing.

'Let me get this as its mine and I wonder how it goes there my mobile phone' she looks at the grass in the forest and sees her mobile phone.

So as she answers the phone and then hears the sound of a voice she recognises as it's the girl she fears the most who bullies as in jenny maycourt rat who is better none outside of earth as princess munryeits in her blue skinned elves self.

'Give me the necklaces it Abigail or you will die and tell me were you are or will kill both your parents, and that madding android boyfriend of yours prince Freddy as you have caused me all sorts of trouble '

'I can't give you it as it mine and please promise me you wont hurt them and by the way Freddy not my boyfriend '

so on the hexagon space craft princess munryeits laughs at her by saying 'so according to legend and modern and future sayings it says you get close to Freddy and I wonder if you are that thorn in the flesh enemy of mine microcosmic girl as if I found you are hiding her from me you will be very sorry indeed spot face as you are very ugly and so stupidity as have tracks you down to fairgoer as you better give me it or your parents and Freddy will die at my hands as I don't take prisoners as you must now be by now as I wont stop until you give me what is rightfully mine as I need so I can rule the galaxy as my father has promised me the milky way galaxy to rule as a warrior princess forever'

at that Abigail puts switches of the phone and throws it away and within hours later as Sedrac takes Abigail to cranbrayort city the capital of flairegore to the royal castile of king raja and queen mesrhea before night falls.

Princess Munryeits arrives in clemnoc forest.with her troops of red robed blue skinned elves and she her troops slaughter the entire horde of unicorns as she and her troops hunt them down.

She picks the mobile which Abigail tossed on the floor and looks at the hoof foot prints of the contour on the grass.

She points at it and summons up her troops 'we must follow the footprints as I am sure she is ridding on her the back of it as men gather forth and make yourselves legends as I can smell her blood and we are not to far as men gather up some horses for yourself as we are going to capture her and that contour and soon the declass and this world and many worlds will be mine forever'

So princess munryeits follows the foot prints.

04
THE TIME PORTAL DOORWAY

So the troops see Abigail and sedarc in the city next to the castile and they move in very slowly towards them as they gallop on horseback towards them and georef gets very excited thinking it's the unicorns which has followed him out of the road to the road outside the castile leading to it,

He looks round and see over five thousand red robed men on horseback with laser guns firing blank shoots into the air as princess munryeits

Tells her troops not to hurt them yet as she needs them alive and to fire warning shoots at them.

Sedarc runs as fast as he can with Abigail riding on his back in the road way of the outskirts of the city which has lots of cottage houses.

The troops of the princess manage to teleport a net on the grind in the forest and grab hold of it as they enter the road way and lots of people in the city hear the

Noise of the troops and see the troops lead by princess munryeits on a white horse enter the city with a net of which to they throw over sedarc and Abigail riding on her back.

Very soon king ramjax and his men come riding in the city on flying horses with laser swords and gather around the troops of princess munryeits as her troops back off to a open field of grass.

The elderly king who has grey hair and a white beard points at princess munryeits and yells with the Top of voice 'what is the meaning of this as we have sight peace with your father zarn as this is a act of war to invade my land and entrap my servant who is keeper of the unicorns and a mere human girl as speak munryeits for yourself as why have come to falireogore to disturb our peace 'says the elve king

Princess Munryeits out of respect for the elve king who has silver skin

Which glows orbiting light rays as his race is none as the on tore. She then bows her head down and says with a soft voice out of respect.

'I today sign a truce with you majority ramjax the great that and my father the

Emperor are not interested in invading your world as we are after this human who has what is mine and in the process of us chasing after her the unicorns got lose and sadly got on our war as I am telling you the truth as it's the girls necklace I really want as she has what truly belongs to me as its mine and she and her friends from the future steal it from me as I only want what is mine as daddy will go mad if he found I had it stolen by her friends in the future as I have travelled from the future to get it back as the necklace is no good to wear for a mere mortal human but must be worn by a immortal like my self.

As surly you must understand the importance of this as this human is very dangerous as she is a witch and must be burnt at the stake like all witches as she has cast a spell on your servant as you can see'

So sera tryst to comfort Abigail as she bursts into tears afraid of princess merits who wants to take her necklace away and of the troops as well as the flying horses.

'dear dear she wont hurt you and you are no witch as no witch has been seen on her world for centuries as if any one is a witch its you munryeits 'Abigail looks away as the princess walks towards her and grabs the necklace of her neck and the necklace chain breaks and then the computerised symbiotic necklace

Then speaks to Abigail.

'transmutation aborted until host can repair or water of tunac is used to heal transmutation or now as to dangerous as to transmute as were is the host as transmutation symbiotic microcosmic girl seeks suitable host who only can repair' so princess munryeits presses a button on the disc that's on the symbiotic necklace and a glass of water appears out of nowhere on the ground.

So the king says 'I have seen enough please leave my world '

Princess Munryeits who is dressed in dark black robes looks at the water and then at Abigail who looks at sedarc then the king who smiles at the young eleven year old girl.

'this is tunac water for the gods to drink and no human a mortal who has stolen from a god can drink from it as this will prove that the necklace belongs to me as if you want it back Abigail or should I say shinny spot face as I say to you in my human self you must dual with me with the sword or at laser point gun but if they you are to afraid to take me on then it proves you are a thief a real thief who must head back to earth as a mortal'

As Abigail slaps the princess across the face as it's the first thing she has done to the shape shifting blue skinned elve who is none on earth as jenny maycourt.

As in bravery but the princess then shoves her to the grass and then the princess drinks of the glass of water which cause the chain to heal it self and she gets one of her men to put the necklace around her neck and suddenly the symbiotic starts to speak 'host as accepted as princes Alicia jenny munryeits maycourt'

So princess munryeits bows her head again to the king who see with own to eyes what has happened and then speaks to her in a soft tone 'ok leave our world as I will deal with the human girl but remember this is a act of war as you have killed my unicorns'

'what about our peace treaty as daddy does not want to war with falireogore as you have aerial advantage on horse back but remember she got in the way so why not agree upon a truce to get her home to earth and once she is home we can do start a war as if you want then I am willing as I have army so vast it can engulf your world in seconds but lets take her home as she is out of her depth her dealing with immortals like us'

So the king goes towards Abigail and gets her off the grass as sedarc stands beside her to defend her from the princess.

'Sedarc I want you when we leave to take her to safety to the time portal gate as me in case many others pursue her here as must head back to earth as I am sure she will be looked after more readily by her kind '

So the princess gets of her horse so the men and all teleport aboard the space mother ship the hexagon.

So the king walks towards Abigail and looks at her face which glows and takes look at her mole on her face.

'human girl you face omits rays like one of us and I wonder if you are a Ontore like us maybe your parents are Ontore as we Ontore on fairgoer glow quite a lot and I have never seen it in a human child with small ears compared to our pointed ears and I must ask you about powers without the necklace'

Abigail looks at the king who wants to understand how comes a human girl omits light rays from body including the face.

'I have strange powers I cant control and with the necklace it harnesses my powers and its why I want to go home to contact general solrac in private as he will no what to do about my necklace as it was given to me by her a strange girl in a green and black costume with a helmet visor on and she was tall'

So the king touches her face to feel the mole on her face and then at her braces on her teeth as she smiles at the king.

'so you say you were given it but how comes princess munryeits claims its hers as it must be stolen and how would crate such a device for the hands of a dark princess who none other than a sorceress and I had no option but to let her take it off you as I need to be sure it really belongs to her '

Sedrac puts hands to Abigail's who is now very tearful as she wants to go home and wants the necklace back as it gave her most courage

the king hands Abigail a silver tissue paper to wipe her tears and then ask one of his men to take her to the time portal door 'take her to thee doorway to earth as this doorway will take her home and Sedrac I am assigning you a new duty as Procter and keeper of the doorway as I should be cross with you for allowing the unicorns to be killed as gerbash the gate keeper of time is very frail due a curse out on him a witch and we need new hands to guard the time portal as I have decided there is no need for much council about the girl but of war with anzorerites who have killed our unicorns please take her home Sedrac were she belongs on earth with her kind'

So the king departs on his flying horse with his men and leaves Abigail with Sedrac who walk towards a stage wooden door on a large fat tree sheared by a glowing elve man with a white beard and greyish hair.

Sedrac hands gerbash the portal time gate keeper a scroll as the king had scroll written up commanding Sedrac to take her home.

Sedarc heads towards the elderly man who reads the scroll and then points at the well that's a few yards from the tree gateway door.

'you must drink the waters of eternity Sedarc together with the girl as it will safeguard you against evil and bring you were you want to go as I have the keys of time to many worlds including earth and when you leave here you must lock the door behind you as it will keep out strangers to our world as the gateway to earth is long tunnel of light and I have the keys to get you to earth but be aware of the dangers their as the king has written we are at war so go on you centaur and you human girl who glowed like us on tore on flaigore '

so gerbash gets a key from his robes and it changes shape and the bottom, of the key looks like a planet like earth and gerbash hands the small key and the other set of keys with small round ball which represent planets to Sedrac who opens the door and they see a bright light like the sun at the end of the tunnel which has lots of lintels on it and Abigail at first is scared to go in until Sedrac reassures her it's the way to earth.

So they walk along the tunnel and head in to a time whirlpool which moves them about as the light from the sun the anti gravity moves them about in a circle and within a few minutes Abigail finds herself in her bedroom with Sedrac who activates the time key by walking towards a black door and her opens it and Abigail is home.

Sedrac hands a key to another world a green and silver key and tells her 'this planet is were I will be as there is gate their that has no guard and it is were you will find me as I must seek some unicorns as I wonder if there is any on go tour were the dwarves live and I cant enter earth as I will be killed and hunted down by men as its not safe place for a centaur to be so farewell argil for now and remember you have powers without the necklace as you for me are microcosmic girl the rightful host of the symbiant '

So Sedrac departs from her room and she sees the black door on the pink wall in her room disappear into thin air as Sedrac heads of to another world in search of unicorns.

05
THE INTERLACT SPACECRAFT

So Abigail heads downstairs to the livening room and to her horrow she finds that her mother lying in a pool of blood with a note on the table written by her killer.

'I told you I would kill your mother and any who stand in my way as thanks to you we at war and I ready for war with any who stand in my way '

So Abigail dials her mobile phone and to general solrac the frogman who answers the phone 'abbey were have been your parents the school the cosmic police as well as mi5 and mi6 and Interpol also the cosmic police force have

Looking for your whereabouts and that of your kidnappers and please tell me what the criminals

And were you as your father has as been waiting for some news since your kidnapping

Abigail then breaks down in tears and tells the frogman general that her mother has been killed 'so I am heading straight to you with the

Cosmic council police and men from Scotland Yard please don't touch any thing as we it as evidence to find out who did this'

So within hours the cosmic military police turn up as well as the army and civil police officers from Scotland Yard.

They question her and so does the frogman general who then hearts from a tearful and very angry Abigail 'I am going after her to gain vengeance for my mothers death and for recovery of the necklace given to me which has strange powers and turns me into someone else '

So soon her father Tim comes home and sees Abigail in tears being hugged by a frogman and he then hugs as the police tell him that his wife has been murder by an evil killer who was kidnapper of her daughter.

The house in bloom bury road is cordoned off and no one allowed in as the worlds media tell of the murder of Pam fryler the funeral takes place and its during the funeral with Abigail in dark dress that Abigail speaks to her father about having a break from school for a while maybe a week or to so she can grave her mothers death as well as help catch her mothers killer.

Her father who has fair hair tall and thin

To go to school but she says that she will be bullied by the killer.

At her school jenny may court shows up after missing a few

Few weeks and the police confront her about the kidnap ands she uses her telepathic powers to convince police is she is innocent

Of the kidnapper as the murderer of Abigail mother Pam.

In one evening Abigail contacts the general who is keen for her sign up as a cosmic military secret agent in search of princess munryeits and the necklace.

So the general turns up one afternoon when her father is at work and her aunt Hilary in the kitchen answers the door and lets the general in.

'we have a big problem as the keys to earth have been stolen and some one has used a symbiotic being to open a large portal in hidey park and our men have cordoned off the area saying to the media it's a gas leak but it wont hold for long as members of the media have got past our cordon and have ask have asked questions

About the humming noise coming from Hyde park which keeps residents awake at night as our men have done all the best to shut the portal but it wont shut without the right keys to the doorway so its why I am here to tell you '

so her aunt Hillary who is looking after Abigail while she takes time off school gets the fright of her life when she see a tall and fat frogman in the room dressed in military uniform.

'Who are you and what are you as I cant remember seeing around here' she falls on

the floor and soon comes round only to find out that Abigail and the frogman have disappeared as they teleport abroad a space craft and round sphere ship that's white and as the interlact look a an weather balloon from far off as earths military have seen vessel like it and call them weather balloons.

'I hope Aunt Hillary is ok '

So aboard space. Ships she sees plasma screen of earth and looked at the space ship bridge area were she sees Freddy Dothan the android prince.

As well as a white dove bird speaking to Freddy which is Abigail's pet dove metra

Was teleported on board as well?

So the general shows her around the space time ship which has eight bedrooms a kitchen a living room area and seating next to the cockpit area.

In the bridge there is four chairs on sliver carpeted floor with white metal walls a dash board which has buttons and throttles at all as the ship is operated by a person putting cotter pin device in the mind that made by a probe which places a pin like device in the mind which also acts as universal translator.

So Freddie tells the computer on the vessel to head to goytoour the planet of the dwarves.

On parallel they are finding themselves seeing giants all round the landscape of Claremore and no dwarves in sight as some how the landscape is empty of dwarves.

06
THE DWARF SLAVES

In the work house kitchens and factories on goytor a full of small houses and trees in the land the dwarves are kept as slaves and a boy none as claytor a dark haired dwarf

boy who has pigs snout and pigs tails and red horns like most of the goytocks and elderly dwarf man none as Kelvin o riley are chained to a giant kitchen sink were they wash lots of giant cooking pots and pans and a dark giant who is head chef and unchains them and then whips and chains to giant gas cooker which has lots of ladders all over and as giant chefs open the door to ovens dwarves fall off.

'I want you two to peal some vet with your bar nails and pot the opiates and carrots into pot and if you done I will throw you in for supper to be eaten by our guests.

' you will be sorry one day giant as one day we will be free and you will be killed by the dragon people as they eat giants for supper

' says the hairy dwarf man who wears green robes and hat on his head as he leprecorn none as

The dwarf boy is a native of goytor but unlike other dwarfs the goytocks don't grow beards unlike other dwarves who grow beards

'we will never be free as there is no won willing out third in the cosmic coin ill to save us as they don't know us being slaves' says the dwarves boy

A mile away in the field giants surround the space ship and lead by very tall giant as

Perec the great the leader of the giants.

'any ortbeings one who trespasses were I rule will be taken to the work houses as slaves to cook our meals and bake bread made out if human bones as smell a human girl here as girl come to be or I will crush you and give to my bakers to make bread with.

he sees an attired boy and pulls off one of prince ferries arm off and Abigail gets very scared as the giant leader none as Perec the great a very large giant who is taller than all the other giants and is tall as skyscraper as the other giants reach up to his knee and are like dwarves to him as the crendor are giant dwarves and Perec the great lifts up Abigail into his huge gigantic hands.

'you done smell like a human but hot bony elve and I no what I will do to you I will make a servant to my wife who needs a elve to make her dresses for evening meals out at the restaurant I wont eat you yet as long as you make a nice dress for my wife.

Prince Freddie puts back his robotic arm in the socket and takes out erratic screw driver and is seen doing by a goldsmith for the giants 'you machine boy I want you as my slave to make large gold bars so I can build a palace of gold reaching space'

The giants try to lift up the interlact but they fins they can't as it's too heavy for them as Prince Freddie puts a force field around it keeping it on the ground.

General Solrac remains on the vessel as he tells Freddie that he will remain on board and hides under a table in the dining room of the space vessel. As giants try to lift up the spacecraft.

'A giant rushes toward the gigantic leader of the giant

'Perec sir we need more slaves for the kitchens as we are short slaved at the moment as I cant find any more dwarves At that Perec bends down at the smaller giant and hands him Abigail and picks up the android boy prince from the grass.

The smaller giant puts them in a giant black sack and heads to beavemont city were all

the mostly live and were almost all the goytocks are as in the city their gigantic horses with carts and gigantic wells were giant women take water of wells using giant buckets and some which carried by hundreds of dwarves.

So the small giant takes them out of his gigantic black sack and puts chains them and takes them to a gigantic house to a kitchen. And he chains them onto the top of the cooker and gives them giant potatoes and carrots to peal with weave nails from dead dwarves.

As dwarves nails are very sharp as dwarves unlike the goytocks.

'Abbey pass me yours as yours looks sharper than mine' says the android boy.

So she passes to the dwarves nail to him and then he hands it back to her and Abigail blushes at the good looking android boy whom she has crush on looks at the android prince with

Wonderment at him and as he manages to peel the vegetables very fast and she cant stop blushing and she goes all pink due her blushing at him as he looks like a sixteen year teenage boy.

The giant head chef then whips Abigail with a whip and then yells' hey human girl why don't you work like this machine here as you are to slow and you no what we do with slow ones' says the giant who makes Abigail cry so much that her tears turn to blood and within minutes she gets so upset that she cuts her hands.

The giant looks at her picks up and holds her down wards from the legs to make her tears hit the cooking pot the giant laughs at her so much that it makes the android prince angry and he throws the nail at the giant hitting his eye and he drops Abigail and she when almost dropping to the kitchen floor summons her necklace off princes munryits who appears out of nowhere laughing unwire that the necklace has despaired from her neck as Abigail see in the ground and pointing a wand at the giant who cant see her as she puts spells on the giants to make them not her but Abigail and prince Freddie see her laughing below.

As the andiron looks again at the grind she becomes invisible.

Princess Munryeits stands next to the giant as she is invisible unwire the when Abigail is near the symbiotic necklace she can sense its presence and it's why she summons it to disappears off her neck and go on her neck.

'I summon you necklace to leave the princess acetate Abigail fryler myself as your host to leave the princess' says

So turns into microcosmic girl and within seconds she changes into the green cat suite and green vial wearing superhero girl and she flees upwards and punches the head chef in the groin.

'Are it hurts and I will get you for that for hurting me human.'

'hey you will die for this human girl as you will used as starter as we like to have human girls for starter as I have seen one that can fly without wings as I will make you pay for what you did and you machine boy 'says the giant

The dwarves in the kitchen see whets happening and Kelvin the elderly dwarves man throws lifts up a giant opiates peeling and throws it the grind as a giant head chef gets out his whip to sort microcosmic girl who fires blue rays from her hands stun rays but he is to big to stunned but gets a tickling feeling and starts to scratch him so much he drops the whip the dwarves in the work house kitchen stop working and start to rebel by throwing their peelings and drop cooking pots and pans as thousands upon thousands of dwarves

Who are in the kitchen and they all start cheering microcosmic girl as she fires a ray at his eyes which make blind for a few minutes.'

'look a I cant I cant see I cant see and were you human girl as when I find you I will turn you grind your bones into flour to make bread with '

The other giant chefs get out their whips to make the dwarves go back to work and

microcosmic girl unchains them by firing laser rays from her hands which break the chains and she gets the giant keys that lock the chains of the giants and then fires rays at the eyes of the six other giants in the kitchen and the dwarves run out of the kitchen chassed by the giants who get their sight back so the giant chef gets his whip and hits microcosmic girl with hit and crash lands on a cooking pot next to the giant washing up sink and dishwasher.

She dents the sink and water starts to leak out the sink which is full of water and as the giant rushes over to grab her with his giant hands he slips over the wet floor of the kitchen and pile of giant cooking pots that's full of washing up liquid and water hit on the head and make him all wet and he goes he becomes unconscious and falls asleep.

So soon the dwarves of guitar all start to rebel against the giants egged on microcosmic girl who aides them in escaping and the giants start to get very confused and scared as the dwarves who out number them gather all round so the dwarves all gather round the giants and throw mud into their eyes using catalysts and the frogman hears the noise of the dwarves faint the giants helped by microcosmic girl while on the interlact space craft that he comes out and sees giants ruining away from the lilted people who out number them and they head of to a giant door way a red door in giant tree that's been planted by giants a which is space portal to their home world of crendor that's full of giants like themselves.

Microcosmic girl finds her power fading as the necklace Disappears from her and she changes back into Abigail fryler and sees princes munryeits wearing the necklace again of she grabbed of her a few days ago.

As princes munryeits becomes visible and she taunts Abigail with venomous words

'you may have defeated the giants but wont me as I am very powerful and I wait your death as I will become eternal forever and a goddess and I will rule the galaxy as nothing can stand in the way of the dark side' says the princes and it makes Abigail cry.

So the princess disappears into thin leaguing her head off as she wears the symbiotic necklace and dwarves all gather a around Abigail and wonder at the human girl crying and a wave boy none as claytor looks at girls face and says' its you as I had day dream about meeting you human says the dwarves boy who is like a native on goytor as he has a pigs nose and pigs tails also pink horns on his head.

v byleaf my mother a goytor concubine to the king during the war we lost as they are to big for us and I thank you for what you did as I have herd of humans but seen one in my life and I would love to go to earth to see more of your kind as I have herd a have half sister who came to earth and you like her as I have seen your before In the cosmic gazette as you are arcadia microcosmic girl my lost sister so can I come to earth with you sis'

'I'm sure you can come to earth with us says Abigail.

'About me my name is Abigail not arcadia your half sister as I may look like her and may be mistaken anyway some call me abbey for short' says Abigail

So prelaare the leader of the giants comes throw the door with a whip to make the dwarves return to work as he does the dwarves fire giant stone from catapult and hits Perec on the head killing him instantly and the dwarves throw are party to celibate the giants leaving their world and heading to giant portal door of which is shut by Sedrac the cantor who shuts the door way that's in a giant tree leading to their world and general solrac tells the dwarves to cut down the tree.

07
THE FRIENDLY GIANT

So later that day general solrac heads back to the interlact space craft with Prince Freddie, Abigail. Sedrac the centaur and claytor who begs them to take him to earth so he can meet humans also meet the queen of England.

'Let me go with you as I must go and see the human race on earth '

So claytor who is outside the spaceship as Abigail and the genaal.are about to head into the sloppy ramp leading the white glowing vessels a sphere shaped vessel which is also time machine space vessel and her follows them on board and finds the vessel very big inside as its also time and inter dimensional vessel were its larger in the inside and he follows

On board and the general snaps with anger at the goytocks dwarf boy.

'We have no time for tourists 'says the angry frogman.

'But abbey please tell him please tell him abbey to allow me to come to earth with you so can meet humans' says the dwarves boy.

Soon out of nowhere the pronounces munryreits appeared with a giant under a spell as she points her ortlare stick at him and presses a button and chants the words 'hectpe mylork hecot myork hecott mylortk' and he takes club from the floor left by the giants to beat dwarfs with 'kill them all and bring her to me as she will be slave until she dies' so the giant who has red hair and reddish beard takes a club to beat the frogman with and Freddie who hears the voice of the evil princess and Sedarc gallops about and knocks the giant man georef on the ground and some how the spell is broken and she gets a whip to whip the giant with and hits his knee 'you will crush them gebore as you under my power and control 'so she chants a few words of magic but it fails to work on him as she points her ortlare stick at him and he looks at Abigail who is crying as she more terrified of the giant than princes munryreits who holds a wooden club that's shaped like baseball bat in his hands .

'Don't kill me giant as I am a good girl really and I have a necklace that she is wearing '

Says Abigail to the girl in the grass area of the land norgork on the planet gotock was there are lush tree and a farm yard in the distance with cows grazing on the grass.

'gebor not bad giant but good won he doe hurt human girl but will hurt elvy girl princes for making gebor bad giant as gebor nor kill no one as gore not like by me people who are bad giants and thet kill off al l of all of tbaybeings what is name hormain girl 'says the giant who starts to become friendly with her

Abigail raises a smile as Sedarc gallops on the ground with front feet coming up at the princess who drops her metal electronic wand none as an ortlare stick.

'My name is Abigail and please don't hurt me will you giant 'says the human fair haired girl.

'gebore dun t hurtsis abitsgail as he is good giant and want be fends with abitsgail as gebor cant hurt human girl as gebor comes form line good mutes and is only good giant now as other good ones and kill good ones and elvy the king help me escape I come to gate to fight others like me who bad ones and princess took me to her world to but gebor say no and I was bringer her by princes with machine wand and centaurs is brave warriors worth bad princess as good princes I meet as you like angel princess of the sky she tell of gebore for eating meat as gebor is bad to eat meat say sky pinches as you like sky princess who can fly as it abairtsgail angry with gebore' says the red haired giant.

'You fool bring her to me at once or I will turn you in to mob 'says the evil princess

As it gets dark and the distance and noise of wild wolves is herd.

At that claytor gets scared 'these parts are none for dangerous wolves and I hate wolves as they bite says the dwarf'

'Gebor want s to be friend with wave boy and horseman and you abitsgail '

'Her name is Abigail you fool as cant you speak promptly as I am fed with your stupidness '

Says the evil princes.

'gebor stupid giant as others call me stipid but gebor claver he do kill or punish dwaefys

No one but will hurt elvy wicked princess' so rushes toward her she and Sedarc take out swords and gebor knocks on the ground.

At claytor grabs hold of her laser sword and points it her and she finds herself surrounded as georef. Sedarc, price Freddie, Abigail and the frogman all gather round her.

'Surrender or die by your own sword munryreits 'says the frogman

'never as I don't listen to frogman or other non anzore as I will turn you all into mob or leave you all to the wolves' she then blows into a whistle very loudly and wild wolves appear out of nowhere next to them prince Freddie fight them of using a giant whip and general solar gets pulls out his laser gun as for Sedarc he jumps at them.

So Abigail seizes the chance to pull the necklace of the princess neck and she changes into microcosmic girdle and tells the others 'let me deal with her and the wolves alone as I fight alone and need no protection form her witchcraft as I am me '

So as microcosmic girl is about to use her sword to fight her with the evil princess pulls hard at her hair and grabs the necklace from her and while the princess has the necklace Abigail who power is starts to fade takes of her vial and the wolves run off as they surround the giant a pack of six wolves and she changes back into Abigail she chases them by fireing rays from her hands the wolves then run off scared and suddenly princess munryreits disappears again with the necklace.

Abigail collapses on the floor and is lifted by gebor and she wakes from her brief unconscious but is very weak and Prince Freddie the android takes out a small scanning device which read radiation.

'she is dying unless we take her to mount seebrace on flairgore were there is length cosmic force coming from the higher realms she will die from radiation as she must wear the necklace until she is aged eighteen were she may drink of the fountain of eternal youthhood and become immortal as it will her immortal again as she is dying 'says the android.

The other gather round her and gebor hand her to the frog man who carries her on his arms and places on a bed in the space ship.

'Don't die sis as you are my sister abbey and ramjax is your real father and I love you so don't die as we are going to earth and we can meet the queen of England' cries the dwarf boy.

'Machine stick will save abitsgail as gebore seen is it cure others in princess world who is ill'

Says the friendly giant who manages to squeeze himself on board the vessel

And he takes up most of the room on board the space craft as he is far too big.

'We are dropping you at crendor were your kind belong' says the very angry frogman who is squashed between him and the cockpit bridge door.

'I now why not teleport to mount seebrace in flairgore as now the coordinates of the planet 'says the android.

The frogman snap with an angry croak in his voice 'we have no room in here as I cant breath and lets him go and head to the portal gate to his world before its destroyed by the dwarves ' says the centaur

'ok gebor upset as he herd of mount and want to be small being not biff as gebore wail head to gate to go home to fight   bad giants as they kill all of good mutes on gebor world 'so gebor leaves with tears in his eyes and looks at the space ship and shouts out loud so they all here 'look after abitsgail look afar please abitsgail for me and make he live and visit me in gebor world' cries the giant loud who tears cusses a flood to happen as he cries and cries and cries and cries as he heads to the portal gate were the dwarfs are still cutting down the tree .

'here look theirs a giant who is crying and we must contact princess arcadia 'says silver skinned woman dwarf who giving out cakes and buns to dwarf workers as thousands of them saw away at hack with saws at the giant tree they stop working to eat and due it rating down tears from the giant who heads into the broken cosmic door way in the tree the red door which lead into a portal to his world that's full of giants.

The dwarves all cheer as he enters he enter though the door war and mangoes to yell out loud 'abitsgail the homnon girl dying all becose gebore stipid giant 'says gebore.

Later on that night the dwarf's manatee to cully cut down the giant tree which led to passage way into the giant's world of crendor.

08
SEEBRACE MOUNTAIN

So the interlact arrives on flairgore near mount seebrace in the valley of mescal Abigail is held in the arms of the frogman fast asleep and very close to death he followers the adios prince who leads the way to hill top of mount of seebrace of were there is lightning coming from the sky and the mountain has a volcano and lave comes from the volcano.

Abigail wakes up and wonders wear she is as she loses her memory of being microcosmic girl and of who the frogman is 'hey get me down and who are you as you look like a frog who is a man' says Abigail.

The frogman croaks and smiles at her as she looks at him with wonderment at the android at also the centaur and dwarf boy.

' you are not human and I must be damaging or some kind of world as how did I get here as I never seen such a bunch of freaks as I tight I was weir with my mole and my glow on my face but this must be a dream. As who are you freak anyway as why here'

She utters in her deep breath at them.

'she is going insane as she cant remember us and it's the radiation its getting to her mind and unless we take her quaky to the top she will die as munryreits has the necklace and its her only chance by taking to the top of the mountain to reach the door to the higher realms of ort alpha as very few been their and legend says it's the door war to heaven as it her only chance of living as gebor let her ride to the hill the hill top on your back'

Says the android

'I won't ride on freaks back and don't you look familiar as somehow I feel I no you from somewhere' says Abigail.

'its from the very long past and its very long story and anyway trust me if you want to go home you have to head to top of the hill and head downwards to a door way to earth and to your dad'

'I must be dreaming 'she collapses on the floor as the air runs thin as they walk up hill of mount seebrace Sedarc has her on his back unconscious.

'She is dying and we are to late' says the frogman.

'don't die abbey wake up wake up sis 'he restates her from blowing breath from his mouth into her mouth as he lies on the rock surface of the hill..

'It's no good she is dead 'cries out loud the frogman as he feels her pulse and he burst into tears.

Suddenly a loud noise of a spacecraft about to land in the distance is herd which kind of wakes Abigail up and she gets very scared 'I am still her in this world as I dear hope this is a dream' suddenly appearing out of thin is princess munryreits and some men in black robes who have red skin with scales which glows as it starts to get dark they all have ortlare struck in their hands and are warlocks she yells at them and points at Abigail 'bind them with chains but leave the human girl to me 'so chains come off their wands.

At that Abigail wakes up as claytor revives her and when waking up she sees in the hill a the red skinned girl who has scales on her face and Abigail sees the tall anzore princess change from being azure into to a human girl and Abigail recognises the girl as being jenny' its you and what are doing in my dream'

So the tall girl points her electronic wand at her 'you will die spot face as with you dead I will become immortal again as my powers were darned by your future self as I will become queen of the anzore empire and a cosmic ruler of the univalves that once dad I have taken control of his entire army as you are nothing without this as when I have killed you I will have no need for it as the power from it will flow in my blood and make me immortal forever as I will never taste death as you will Abigail or should I say princess arcadia microcosmic girl as I am taking you to earth to die like your mother and after I have killed you I will open a door way allowing my fleets to enter earth were I will be queen as well as a goddess as have no great power as the power of the darkness runs in my vein and when falls the whole of the universes will be mine' says jenny.

'you are mad and it's a dream and what have I done to you munryeits as it's what they call as my memory of who I am and why I m here as I am not dreaming is coming back as I can feel its cosmic power"

'you will die at my hands arcadia instead on earth men bind with chains and tell commander kwerton I am coming with the king ramjax cherished daughter arcadia microcosmic girl as I have her as it's the day we have all waited for us anozoreites the day the she dies at my hand as its been written about your death as your dearth will mean I can rule the universe "

'I will rule time and soon all this will be mine as I will make my people gods like the immortals of ancient Greece they on tore who travels back to mount Olympus we worshipped instead of this god you call the only god as bunions will pray to me and worship me and I will more followers than your god as wail be a god and the mountain starts to shake as jenny presses a button her ortlare stick to make earthquake happen and jenny grabs hold of Abigail and teleports in to a triangular space craft that's shaped like pyramid that's below the hills.

She tells her men to on the surface speaking to one of her men a field marshal

who has a mobile 'let them burn to death as I want to watch them die form the comfort of the this craft so leave them their while watch them burn with malt and ash' says jenny who changes back into her anzore self but as she speaks to them Abigail pulls the necklace of her neck which has been mended as it cant it can fix self when bracken and when put around a hosts neck

So Abigail grabs hold of it and takes control of the vessel by pointing a laser gun at the ships captain.

'Teleport my friends to the ship or I will have no option but to hurt you 'says Abigail

'Don't you mean kill as I hate these who fail me' so she takes out her wand and kills the ships captain who is a short anzore man.

'you are coming to earth to die with your friends as I toss them out in deep space into airlock as its quick easy death so men teleport her friends to airlock on deck four says the evil princess

So the four or beings are put in a room which has a door which leads to the outside and one the door the operative direction to the inside of the vessels the room is dark and quite smelly due to the smell of vomit as the ashore like the smell of vomit and the whole vessels smells like vomit.

So on the ships cockpit the helmsman pilots the ship to space but as they head to space Abigail grabs hold of the necklace and puts it around her neck and munryits takes out her wand at Abigail who hands her back the necklace.

'Watch your friends die in space as computer open the airlock on deck four' says the princess who dresses in long dark dress and combs her hair while looking at small hand sized mirror on her hands.

'malfunction malfunction airlock on deck four not opening 'says the on board woman's voice of the computer.

'Your majesty we have told a fault with the deck four airlock and the other airlocks 'says one of her men who looks at computer screen.

In the airlock prince Freddie manages to tap into the ships computer by talking to it in computer speech and he tells the computer teleport them to their spaceship on the planet.

'I have grave bad news your royal highnesses say another anzore man looking at monitor in the cockpit area.

'What is it' says munryreits

'The teleportation device has been activated and the prisoners are gone 'says the anzore man who looks at his computer screen in the cockpit area.

'what do you man gone' yells out the princes who holds her ortlare stick at Abigail and puts her away her small mirror into her black handbag and heads over to look at his screen and sees the airlock empty

'ok they wont get far as will command the fleets to seek them out as they wail die by the mighty vessels of the empire' so she gets a phone call from a teenage boy a few light years away on earth and she looks at the screen at the teenage boy 'what do you want eerie as I have to wash my hair as I will speak to you tomorrow' so she presses a button on her mobile and the boy disappears from the screen as he is about to speaks to her.

'Jenny we have a date tonight have you forgotten 'says the dark haired boy.

'Ok make I will try and make it' says the princess

'come to toward and let touch that mole of yours as I will make it hurt you and I will torture you to death with this 'he ortlare struck changes into a laser whip as she presses a button and chants the words 'axeerort hert thy bye' she whips Abigail and blood comes out of her skin as she chains her to a red roving chair in the large cockpit area which is empty.

09
THE RAVEN IN THE NIGHT'S SKY

So the princess speaks to the helmsman while laser whipping Abigail making her cry in pain and blood comes all over her skin and on her white blouse and her blouse gets torn by the whip.

'helmsman take to take to earth to the year 2007 September the 14th midnight in London on near the river Thames as I am going to whip her to death and toss her body in the river

As you will die in shame 'so within hours they arrive in the early twenty first century.

So Abigail is held in chains and taken to the south bank of the river Thames in the waterloo area next to the national theatre their and its midnight when they teleport to the foot path which has riling over looking the Thames and the houses of parliament including big been.

So Abigail is whipped time and time and time again by laser whip and then the princess punts her wand at the sky and speaks to her father emptor zarf on her mobile 'give me permission daddy dear to have your ships celibate the death our cosmic enemy microcosmic girl in a victory slate parade on earth as I want to rule earth'

'ok jenny I allow you this once to have earth but not yet the empire as my spies tell me your plans to oust me form power you can have earth as governor while I rule above your head as empire forever as thank you my daughter for your hares work as its school still for you as the soon to be ruler of earth I want my daughter still to get a good education behind you as a foundation for diplomacy as soon the cosmic council will fall as our fleets have pushed them back in to the lyntor system as jenny make it a quick death for her as you have school tomorrow' says the emperor

'So daddy dearest please just pretty please can I rule other worlds in this galaxy as a crown princess 'says the princess

'you may once you have left school anyway I have some urgent earth business to do as shares in the warlock universes have gone up all thanks to the orate stick as it was souns invention and my company plan to make it global weapon used by law enforcers and the military in the empire so I must love and leave you as I have a dinner with sectos laycroft the king of new Rome as I no you like his son prince eubie who are both on earth on comsic business'

'Yes I do and I was meant to have a date with him but I have her with me and daughter of ramjax in human form as Abigail fryler whom I am going to execute quickly daddy dearest'

'I better leave you to it then' says her father

In deep a fleet of aznore fighter jet space planes attack the interlact before it heads into a wormhole which is space and time inter dimensional door way or portal to other parts of space so the interlact heads to solar system to earth and Abigail who has cuts all over her body looks at the sky the shepherd sphere shaped space craft appeasing out of nowhere as the portal to earths atmosphere opens as the princes punts her ortlare stick at the sky.

So princess munryreits looks up in horror as she sees the interlact fireing laser shoots at her and as she is about to laser whip Abigail to death a laser gun hits her necklace and comes her neck and breaks into two and she points her ortlare stick at it and Abigail grabs it from her hands her weaken state and fight begins the two Abigail pulls at her and she stands back a yard or two and changes into microcosmic girl and it makes the princess very angry with Abigail for having the necklace and changing into microcosmic girl that she presses a button the ortlare stick and chats the words 'borty olds death' and beam of light comes out of her ortlare stick it misses as microcosmic girl moves out of the very quickly due her having her powers back.

The ortlare stick fails to work properly and microcosmic girls fires a ray of blue laser light from her hands at the ortlare stick and as munryeits starts to chant words and she finds heading up in to the sky as microcosmic girl uses her special powers she never she had into making her head off into the portal.

'I am sending you to deep space gift wrapped 'says microcosmic girl

'no you wont I will make you grow old and weak spot face abbey activate device wand growth device and make her grow old and die' so she the button and the spell does not work as it rebounds on her as microcosmic girl puts up a deflector force field round her body a shield that protect from the magic spell from the princess and within a few minutes she starts to grow very old and frail and she finds her self disappearing as she looks at her hands she bones and starts to take her mobile phone to ring her spaceship to beam her board .

They are in deep space and her mobile phone and she puts down her mobile on the pavement

as she panics getting scared as she looks at her hands it changes into bones and soon all her body turns old she grows old whiten minutes and dies and nothing is left of her body apart from her symbiant body which is a raven and it flees off ion the portal and the portal closed after it and Abigail back as her normal self looks at the bones on the floor the crow

bird appears out of nowhere were the bones were as Abigail as microcosmic girl sees no longer the skeleton bones of the princess but a black crow bird on the ground appearing out of nowhere staring at microcosmic girl so it flees off away from Abigail who looks at the bones change into a black raven bird and the bird fly's off into the night's sky heading off into the white light of the round whirlpool portal in the nights sky.

So Prince Freddie, Clayton and the frogman teleport out of the spaceship and see Abigail as herself not as microcosmic girl in tears of what happened.

So the frogman goes up to her and hugs her "dear dear it wail be ok as I saw you use your powers on her and don't worry she wont be back for a while as long as you keep wearing the necklace as it unbounded her spell as its what the necklace was crated for to stop spells from witches and wizards from harming you "

So she looks blankly at the frogman " you are a frogman and who am I as I have no memory of being her or seeing beefier but I feel I no you and can trust you " says Abigail who tears turn to joyful tears.

"You are losing your memory again as it's the necklace its fading and your hair its going all white and crykeee you are growing wings "snaps the frogman

So Abigail starts to grow wings two set of wings one fairy tripe wing and one set of eagle wing like an angel and her she glows very bright like the sun.

So they all bow down to her and she tell them "its me Abigail and do not be afraid as I have no need for the necklace as I am taking it off but will wear it in case she comes back as after all I feel as if I have been around millions of years and now all of you as you are my friends and I feel I have none you all my life since I was a baby "says Abigail.

Suddenly a small little green ortbeing a mutant from ortcosmic city a man who has oval eyes appears out of nowhere and goes up to her and hugs her

"arcadia you have must wait for the dove of god it will find you as its there it will come clavier to you as you are immortal princesses and I am he fellmore the presidential councillor of the cosmic council of worlds so look after her men "he then walks away and then disposers as he does the dwarf boy then hugs her and kisses on the cheeks.

"Sis you were awesome today taking on that witch and you look all heavenly now like always sis "says the dwarf boy.

" but clay I want to be again as I feel all differ and kind of feel very much alive but I want to be abgial again not this as it me as I am all ugly and silly " says abgial tearfully as she feels her wings.

So the adios boy goes up to as Clayton the dwarf boy moves away and as the frogman lights up a fungal leaf cigar and smokes it near the wall that separates the pathway to the river Thames.

"You look fad sis "says the dwarf boy.

"you are not all ugly as we become very close friends you and I abbey and I presses you I will look after you if you want me to that is as not very one takes to me as android elve and I long to be human like you as you may have wings of a fairy and an angel but you are still human "so the android prince takes her hand and kisses it.

" thank you freed its nice of you but I must change back into me again as I have school later on in the mooring and my dad will go livid for being out so late " so she looks at her watch and then she says transmute back with no wings and as a plain urinary school girl from London as after all necklace I am a Londoner and not yet ready for now to be a superhero as its what they call my type aunt it necklace so take me home necklace."

" but abbey we have to go and find the headquarters of the crendodore and stop theses giants from reaching earth and enclosing mankind as I hate giants apart from georef " says the android.

So abgial heads of home and the next she goes to school and sees Georgina on the number forty six bus.

"hey I thought something had horrid had happened to you abbey as you had gone missing as I saw that tall blue man put you in a bag and saw some frogman who told me it was the work of evil or beings from ort alpha anyway your mole its kind got smaller and your spots they have kind of all gone and your face its all bright and shinning and look I see jenny so friends getting on beard but no jenny with them "says Georgina

"They can't hurt me not with her not around as I now of a superhero girl called microcosmic girl who kind of sent her packing into deep space "says Abigail with laughs out loud.

"What do you mean by deep space and microcosmic girl and who is she "says an exited gorging who takes a bar of chocolate and eats it.

"Never mind gorge as long as jenny is not around and my necklace safe that all

That matters "says Abigail.

Lightning Source UK Ltd.
Milton Keynes UK
22 September 2010

160196UK00001B/12/P